Down in Mississippi

Traditional Song Adapted
by Johnette Downing

Illustrated by Katherine Zecca

PELICAN PUBLISHING COMPANY
Gretna 2016

ISBN 9781455620982
E-book ISBN 9781455620999

Printed in Malaysia

Published by Pelican Publishing Company, Inc.
1000 Burmaster Street, Gretna, Louisiana 70053

For my Mississippi ancestors

Down in Mississippi in the surf and the sun lived a mother dolphin and her dolphin one. "Splash," said the mother. "We splash," said the one, and they splashed all day in the surf and the sun.

Down in Mississippi in the Delta blue lived a white-tailed deer and her little deer two. "Prance," said the mother. "We prance," said the two, and they pranced all day in the Delta blue.

Down in Mississippi in a magnolia tree lived a mother mockingbird and her mockingbirds three. "Sing," said the mother. "We sing," said the three, and they sang all day in a magnolia tree.

Down in Mississippi by the ol' lakeshore
lived a mother black bass and her black bass
four. "Eat," said the mother. "We eat," said the
four, and they ate all day by the ol' lakeshore.

Down in Mississippi where the wetlands thrive lived a mother wood duck and her wood ducks five. "Quack," said the mother. "We quack," said the five, and they quacked all day where the wetlands thrive.

Down in Mississippi in the coreopsis lived a mother swallowtail and her swallowtails six. "Flutter," said the mother. "We flutter," said the six, and they fluttered all day in the coreopsis.

Down in Mississippi in a swampland haven lived a mother alligator and her alligators seven. "Snap," said the mother. "We snap," said the seven, and they snapped all day in a swampland haven.

Down in Mississippi in a pond by the gate lived a mother catfish and her catfish eight. "Swim," said the mother. "We swim," said the eight, and they swam all day in a pond by the gate.

Down in Mississippi in a forest of pine lived a mother red fox and her foxes nine. "Leap," said the mother. "We leap," said the nine, and they leapt all day in a forest of pine.

Down in Mississippi in a hive in a glen lived a mother honeybee and her honeybees ten. "Buzz" said the mother. "We buzz," said the ten, and they buzzed all day in a hive in a glen.

Mississippi State Fast Facts

Alligator

Native to the Southeastern United States, the American alligator was chosen as the official state reptile in 2005. Found in freshwater swamps, marshes, rivers, lakes, and bayous, the American alligator is the largest reptile in North America.

Black Bass

Also known as largemouth bass, the black bass became the official state fish on April 12, 1974. Mississippi is home to some of the richest inland water habitats in the United States.

Bottlenose Dolphin

Found in playful pods along the Mississippi Gulf Coast, the bottlenose dolphin was approved on April 12, 1974, as the official state water mammal. In 2008, the Mississippi State Tax Commission approved a *Protect Dolphins* license plate to benefit the Institute for Marine Mammal Studies.

Catfish

Mississippi is considered to be the world's leading producer of farm-raised catfish, since it is reported to produce 60 percent of the world's supply. In 1976, then-governor Cliff Finch named the city of Belzoni the Farm-Raised Catfish Capital of the World, as 40,000 acres of the county within a sixty-five-mile radius are used for catfish farming.

Coreopsis

In 1991, coreopsis (pronounced "cor-ee-OP-sis" and commonly called tickseed) was selected as the official state wildflower of Mississippi. Ranging in color from deep gold to pink, it comprises thirty-five species of perennial, daisy-like flowering plants native to North, Central, and South America. "Coreopsis" is a Greek word for "bug," as the small, dry, flat fruits look like insects.

Honeybee

The honeybee was named the official state insect of Mississippi in 1980. A honeybee hive can have up to 80,000 bees belonging to three castes or groups: queens, drones, and workers.

Magnolia

The Mississippi Legislature officially designated the magnolia, an American native evergreen tree, as the state tree on April 1, 1938, and the magnolia blossom as the state flower in 1952. Known for its showy, large, white blossoms ranging from eight to twelve inches in diameter, the magnolia is a beloved symbol across the state.

Mockingbird

The Women's Federated Clubs and the Mississippi Legislature unanimously chose the mockingbird as the official state bird on February 23, 1944. Mockingbirds have the ability to mimic or "mock" over two hundred songs of other birds and insects.

Red Fox

In 1997, the red fox became one of the two official state land mammals of Mississippi. The red fox, wolf, coyote, and domestic dog all belong to the same family. This omnivore can run at top speeds of thirty miles per hour and leap about seven feet high.

Spicebush Swallowtail

Mississippi approved the spicebush swallowtail as the official state butterfly in 1991. Feeding mostly on spicebush, this slow-flying, pollinating butterfly also feeds on sassafras, camphor, magnolia, honeysuckle, clover, thistle flowers, jewelweed, milkweed, azalea, dogbane, mimosa, and sweet pepperbush.

White-Tailed Deer

Mississippi selected the white-tailed deer as one of the official state land mammals in 1974. White-tailed deer are shy, and when they are startled or sense danger, they characteristically wave their tails from side to side, revealing the white underside. They can run at speeds of up to thirty miles per hour and can swim across large streams and lakes.

Wood Duck

The wood duck was named the state waterfowl of Mississippi on April 12, 1974. Preferring a habitat of woodland areas along lakes, rivers, creeks, and other freshwater vegetated wetland areas, the wood duck is diurnal, meaning that it is active during the day. It sleeps on the water.